The FIRE That SAVED The FOREST

Mike Donahue

Illustrations by Diane O'Keefe

Roberts Rinehart Publishers

Text © 2002 by Mike Donahue
Illustrations © 2002 by Diane O'Keefe

The author and illustrator would like to
thank Barbara O'Keefe, photographer, for the
use of her photographs as reference material for
the illustrations in this book.

Published by Roberts Rinehart Publishers
An imprint of the Rowman and Littlefield Publishing Group
4501 Forbes Boulevard, Suite 200
Lanham, MD 20706

Distributed by National Book Network

Library of Congress Control Number: 2002109723
ISBN 1-57098-420-4 (cloth) and 1-57098-421-2 (paper)
Book design by Ann W. Douden, Boulder, Colorado
Manufactured in the United States of America

Burnie the big Black Bear stood up tall on his back legs and said,

"Without trees we cannot have a forest. . . ."

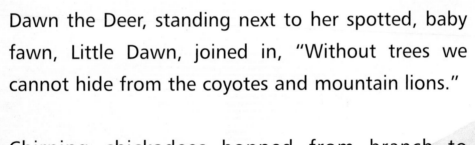

Dawn the Deer, standing next to her spotted, baby fawn, Little Dawn, joined in, "Without trees we cannot hide from the coyotes and mountain lions."

Chirping chickadees hopped from branch to branch and called out, "Without trees we could not have branches to sit on and sing from."

All the animals agreed.
"Trees are the most important part of the forest
and must be saved and protected by every bird
and animal."

Shirley Squirrel planted seeds. Buster Beaver rolled rocks to form a circle of protection around new young trees. Mamma Dawn and Little Dawn Deer were careful not to eat the tiny baby trees. Birds caught beetles that threatened to eat their way into the trees.

And all the birds and animals became a great team of firefighters. "Fire! fire!" Billy Blue Jay squawked. Buster Beaver cut down burning trees. Martha Mouse and Shirley Squirrel put out flying sparks. Burnie Black Bear threw dirt on the flames. Billy Blue Jay and the other birds dropped beaks of water like rain. Together, the animals put out the fires.

Big feasts and great celebrations followed every fire that was put out.

As years went by, new trees grew tall and Little Burnie and Little Dawn grew into Big Papa Bear and Mamma Deer. A new little Burnie Bear and Dawn Deer were born.

Deer hoofs churned up the forest floor helping new seeds to grow. Earthworms chewed up the ground, loosening it up and filling it with air so the tree's roots could grow healthy and strong.

The forest floor became a great carpet of pine
needles. The pine needles added food to the soil
that helped even more trees to grow.
Thick forests grew everywhere.

As more and more trees grew tall, the open grassy meadows became smaller and smaller. The sunlight had a harder and harder time reaching the berry bushes and flowers that grew on the forest floor. Too many pine needles added the right kind of food to the soil for more trees to grow, but the wrong kind of food for berries and flowers and grass to grow.

Her head hung low, ribs pushing out through a thin coat of hair, the hungry Dawn Deer and her thin weak, baby fawn, Little Dawn, struggled through the thick dark forest looking for anything at all to eat.

Up above, quiet birds sat hunched, too hungry and sad to sing. The berries and seeds from the bushes and flowers were gone. Even the trees were having a hard time. No longer were the trees tall and strong and happy. Now the thick crowded trees were thin and short and crammed together. The forest and all its wildlife were dying!

The summer wind was hot and dry and added to the misery of all the birds and animals. High above, in the hot, dry summer air, big black thunderclouds began to form . . . and

CA-BOOOM!!. . .

Lightning struck a dead tree and started a fire.

The animals joined together to fight the fire. But, the animals were too weak, too starved and hungry . . . And the fire was too big! All the years of putting out forest fires had allowed the forest to grow too, too thick with trees. Now there was no way to stop all those trees from burning.

"Run! Run!" they yelled as they used their last energy to get out of the way of the fire. The fire burned and burned until it burned itself out.

Sadly, in a long line, the animals walked through the burned up forest. The world has ended, they moaned. The miserable animals were now even more miserable.

Eventually, with the passing of time, an excited cry came from Dawn Deer. The birds and animals all gathered together to see what Dawn Deer was so excited about. The animals watched as her thin and hungry fawn, Little Dawn, ate the new blades of fresh green grass that had begun to grow in the rich ashes and open space left by the forest fire.

Birds began to sing as they saw berry
bushes and flowers beginning to grow.

With each new spring and summer the big burned out area of the forest fire became more and more alive with meadows, flowers, bushes and clear running streams.

The fire area grew lush with food for all the birds and animals.

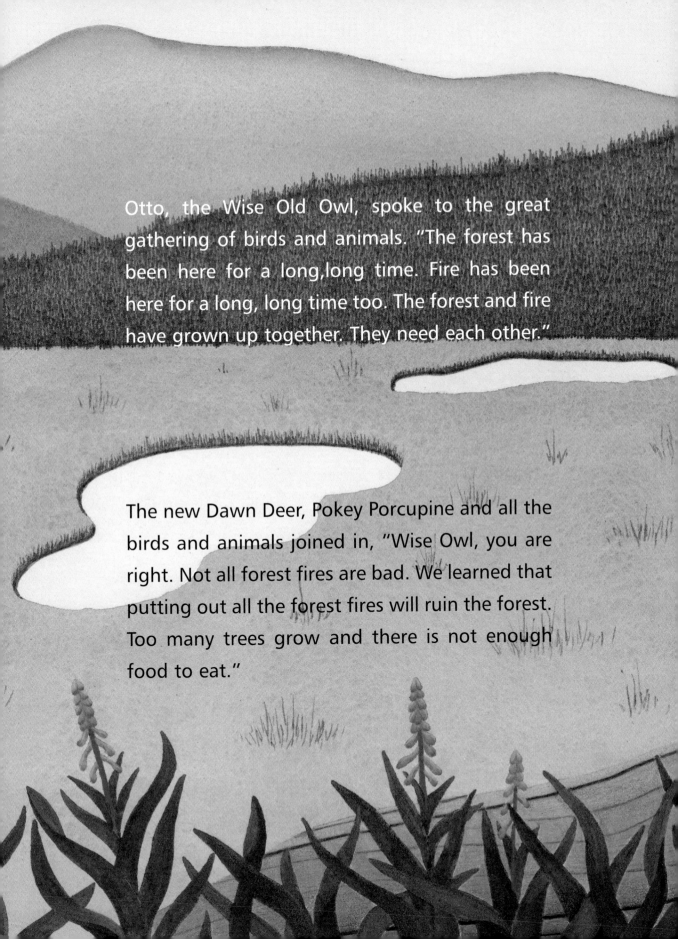

Otto, the Wise Old Owl, spoke to the great gathering of birds and animals. "The forest has been here for a long, long time. Fire has been here for a long, long time too. The forest and fire have grown up together. They need each other."

The new Dawn Deer, Pokey Porcupine and all the birds and animals joined in, "Wise Owl, you are right. Not all forest fires are bad. We learned that putting out all the forest fires will ruin the forest. Too many trees grow and there is not enough food to eat."

The deep, growly voice of the new Big Black Burnie Bear drew all the birds' and animals' attention. The most powerful firefighter of them all stood up to his greatest height, swayed back and forth and spoke out, "I think all of us who live in the forest must give a big thanks to . . .

'The fire that saved the forest.'"

The birds and animals now recognized the importance of forest fires as part of the natural ways of the forest.

TO THE READER:

For more information on the United States government's policy regarding wildfires, including the use of prescribed burns to prevent catastrophic wildfire, readers are urged to consult the U.S.'s official website on the matter at www.fireplan.gov.

Mike Donahue runs the climbing concession in Rocky Mountain National Park, and is the author of the bestselling *Grandpa Tree* (Roberts Rinehart). Diane O'Keefe is a graphic artist living in Denver.